BLOODLINES

A TIME FOR WAR

written by
M. Zachary Sherman

illustrated by
Fritz Casas

colored by
Marlon Ilagan

STONE ARCH BOOKS
a capstone imprint

DEDICATED TO THE MEN AND WOMEN
OF THE ARMED SERVICES

Bloodlines is published by Stone Arch Books, A
Capstone Imprint, 1710 Roe Crest Drive,
North Mankato, Minnesota 56003
www.capstonepub.com Copyright © 2011 by
Stone Arch Books All rights reserved.

Cataloging-in-Publication Data is available on
the Library of Congress website.
ISBN: 978-1-4342-2558-0 (library binding)
ISBN: 978-1-4342-3097-3 (paperback)
Summary: On June 6, 1944, Private First Class
Michael Donovan and 13,000 U.S. Paratroopers
fly toward their Drop Zone in enemy-occupied
France. Their mission: capture the town of
Carentan from the Germans and secure an
operations base for Allied forces. Suddenly,
the sky explodes, and their C-47 Skytrain is
hit with anti-aircraft fire! Within moments, the
troops exit the plane and plummet toward a
deadly destination. On the ground, Donovan
finds himself alone in the Lion's Den without
food, shelter, or a weapon. In order to survive,
the rookie soldier must rely on his instincts and
locate his platoon before time runs out.

Art Director: Bob Lentz
Graphic Designer: Brann Garvey
Production Specialist: Michelle Biedscheid

Photo credits: Alamy: INTERFOTO, 40, World
History Archive, 7; AP Images: U.S. Signal
Corps Handout, 23; Corel, 53; Getty Images
Inc.: Hulton Archive, 52, Hulton Archive/FPG,
41, Popperfoto, 81, Time Life Pictures/George
Rodger, 53; Shutterstock: Olivier Le Queinec,
80; U.S. Air Force photo, 22, 23, SSGT Marie
Cassetty, 73; U.S. Army photo by Himes, 72

Printed in the United States of America
in North Mankato, Minnesota.
052012   006734R

TABLE OF CONTENTS

PERSONNEL FILE

PRIVATE FIRST CLASS
Michael T. Donovan

ORGANIZATION:
Dog Company, 2nd Battalion,
506th Parachute Infantry Regiment

ENTERED SERVICE AT:
Stephens County, Georgia

BORN:
October 2, 1926

EQUIPMENT

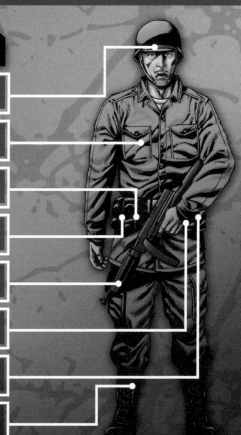

M1C Helmet

M1942 Jacket

M1936 Pistol Belt

Ammunition

Thompson Machine Gun

M1942 First Aid Pouch

.45 Caliber Pistol

Jump Boots

OVERVIEW: WORLD WAR II

In 1939, Adolf Hitler and his German army invaded the country of Poland. This ruthless dictator viewed Germans as the "master race." He hoped to exterminate all Jews from Europe and eventually rule the world. Some countries, including Italy and Japan, joined his evil efforts. They were known as the Axis powers. Others chose to fight against him and his Nazi regime. Those countries, which included Great Britain, France, and the United States, were known as the Allies. To stop German expansion and the genocide of European Jews, the Allied troops could not fail.

ADOLF HITLER

MAP

ALLIED INVASION FORCES

UTAH

OMAHA

Ste Mere-Eglise

GOLD

JUNO

SWORD

Carentan
[DROP ZONE]

Bayeux

FRANCE

Caen

MISSION

Drop behind enemy lines, capture the town of Carentan, France from the German army, and secure an operations base for Allied forces.

CHAPTER 001

THE DROP

Turbulence. A rough ride didn't bother Private First Class Michael Donovan, but the sounds scared him half to death. Every time the C-47 Skytrain hit a pocket of air, the plane shuddered and dipped. The cabin's pop-riveted sheet-metal frame shifted and creaked. Sometimes the noises grew so loud, Private Donovan thought the entire plane would rip apart.

Flying wasn't usually a problem for the newbie soldier — neither was parachuting. He'd already done his mandatory five training "drops." Donovan thought he knew what to expect. Problem was, those parachute jumps had been in clear skies over the Army Camp Toccoa in Stephens County, Georgia. Tonight, soaring 1,500 feet above the black waters of the English Channel, looked and felt a whole lot different.

Mike Donovan, sandwiched between Private Marko Peretti from Philadelphia and Sergeant Frank Anness from New York, looked around at the other passengers. He eyed the nine soldiers of Dog Company, 2nd Battalion, 506th Parachute Infantry Regiment, 101st Airborne, 2nd Platoon. These men were just a few of more than 13,000 Allied soldiers flying toward France in carrier planes.

Their mission: drop behind enemy lines, take Hitler's troops by surprise, and disrupt German operations. Success would allow U.S. troops to land boats, men, and equipment on the beaches of Normandy. It would also create a two-front war for the Germans. With the Americans and British on one side and the Russians on the other, Hitler's troops would be stuck in the middle.

Operation Overlord was the largest invasion in history, and the Allies' first real push into Europe. Everyone from the lowliest grunts to the silver-star generals knew the invasion would succeed. But they had to get there first, and that meant flying through some nasty turbulence.

WHAM! W

Donovan squirmed as the C-47 Skytrain dropped thirty feet in midair and then righted itself. Nervously, he tried shifting in his seat. With more than eighty pounds of gear strapped to his body, moving wasn't easy.

The young private checked his watch. Midnight. Only fifteen more minutes until they jumped — if the planes were on time and in the right place.

Next to him, Sergeant Anness leaned over and smiled. "Don't worry, kid," he said. "We'll get there soon enough!" He glanced down at Donovan's wristwatch. "That's a nice piece! Where'd you steal it from?"

"I didn't steal it," Donovan replied. "My pa gave it to me." He unfastened the watch from his wrist and flipped it over. Engraved on the back casing was a personal message from his father. It read, "Don't count every hour in the day; make every hour in the day count."

"Keep livin' that way, kid," said Sergeant Anness. "And don't you worry, we'll come home again."

"I hope so," said Donovan. He tightened his parachute straps, making sure they were ready to go.

Sergeant Anness frowned. "Didn't you check them straps already, Donovan?" he asked.

"Yes, Sergeant," replied the private.

Anness punched Donovan on the shoulder. "Then leave 'em alone!" he commanded. "Them *Rat-zis* bit off more than they could chew, messing with us."

Donovan looked up at him, concerned. "But what if I can't —?" he began.

"You'll do fine, kid," Sergeant Anness interrupted. "Once we're on the ground, do your job. It's what we're trained for. You get me?"

Donovan nodded. "Got you, Sarge," he said.

KAABOOOM!

A sudden explosion rocked the right side of the aircraft, lighting the midnight sky. The plane dipped violently. All at once, the soldiers turned to the windows, eyeing the black clouds that surrounded them.

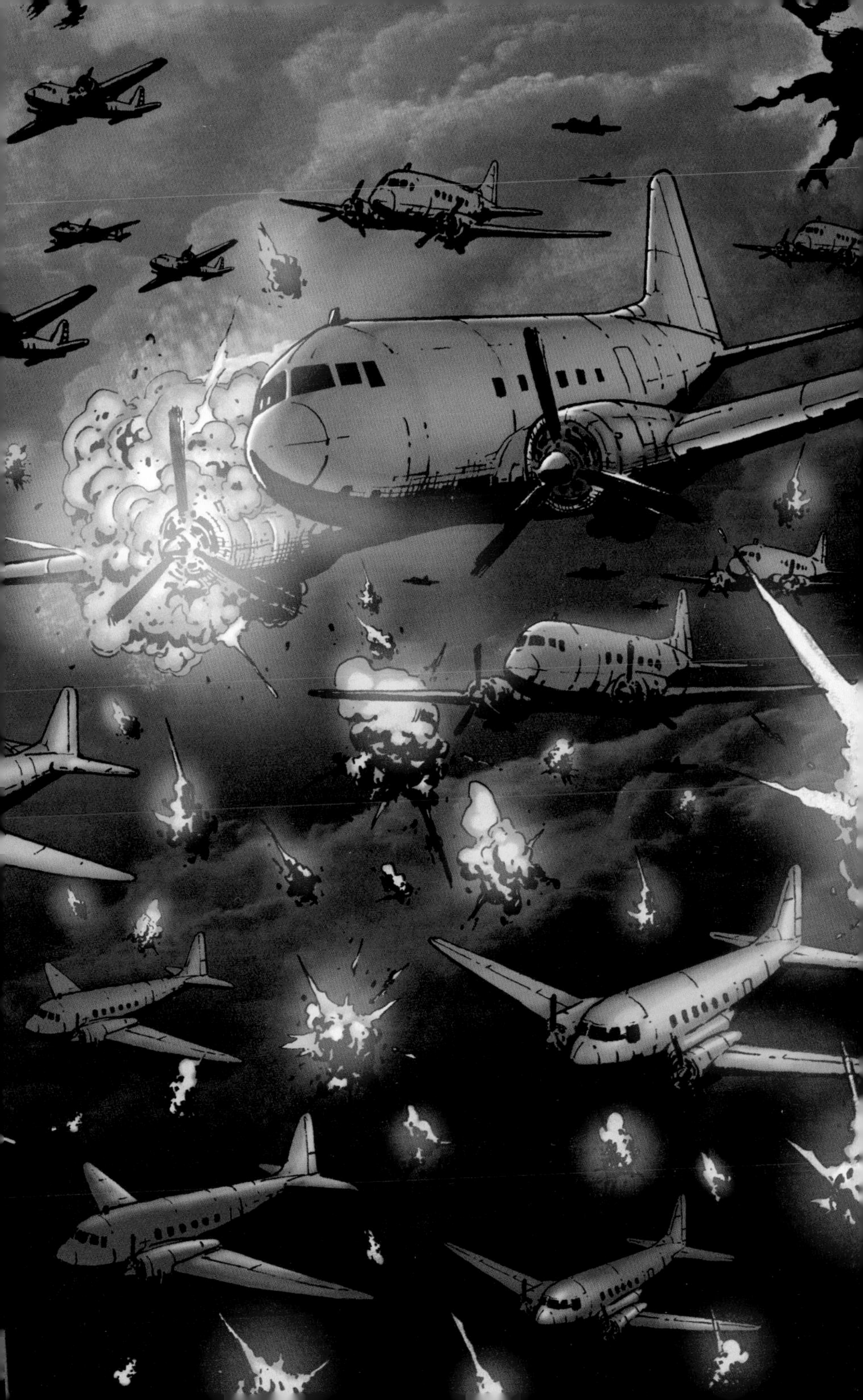

"What is that?!" someone yelled from the front of the aircraft.

"Flak!" answered Lieutenant Spears, shouting over the tremendous explosions.

Turbulence quickly became the least of Private Donovan's worries. The plane dropped once again. Outside, the sky was on fire. Flak pounded the air, and several thousand rounds of German ammunition came at them all at once. A number of the planes, having already been hit head-on, exploded in midair. Others spiraled toward a watery grave in the English Channel, their passengers desperately trying to jump to safety.

For the lucky few still in the sky, landfall was no more than a mile in front of them.

Inside the C-47 Skytrain, the copilot stuck his head out of the cockpit. "Get them ready, Lieutenant Spears!" he shouted.

Suddenly, the cabin turned red as the jump indicator lights came on. The lieutenant rose and waved both hands in the air. Together, his troops stood. At the LT's orders, each soldier checked the gear on the man in front of him. The troops clasped their snap hooks onto the static line above their heads.

Dog Company was ready.

Then the red lights turned green and, one-by-one, men leaped out of the C-47. *WHOOSH!* They were sucked out the door, until finally, PFC Mike Donovan, seventh in line to jump, came to the door and stepped out.

Donovan tumbled through the air. The aircraft was moving too fast! To avoid the weapons fire from the ground, the pilot had accelerated. Unfortunately for the paratroops, this was faster than any of them had ever jumped before.

Finally, Donovan shook away the blurriness. He righted himself, and his parachute fluttered open.

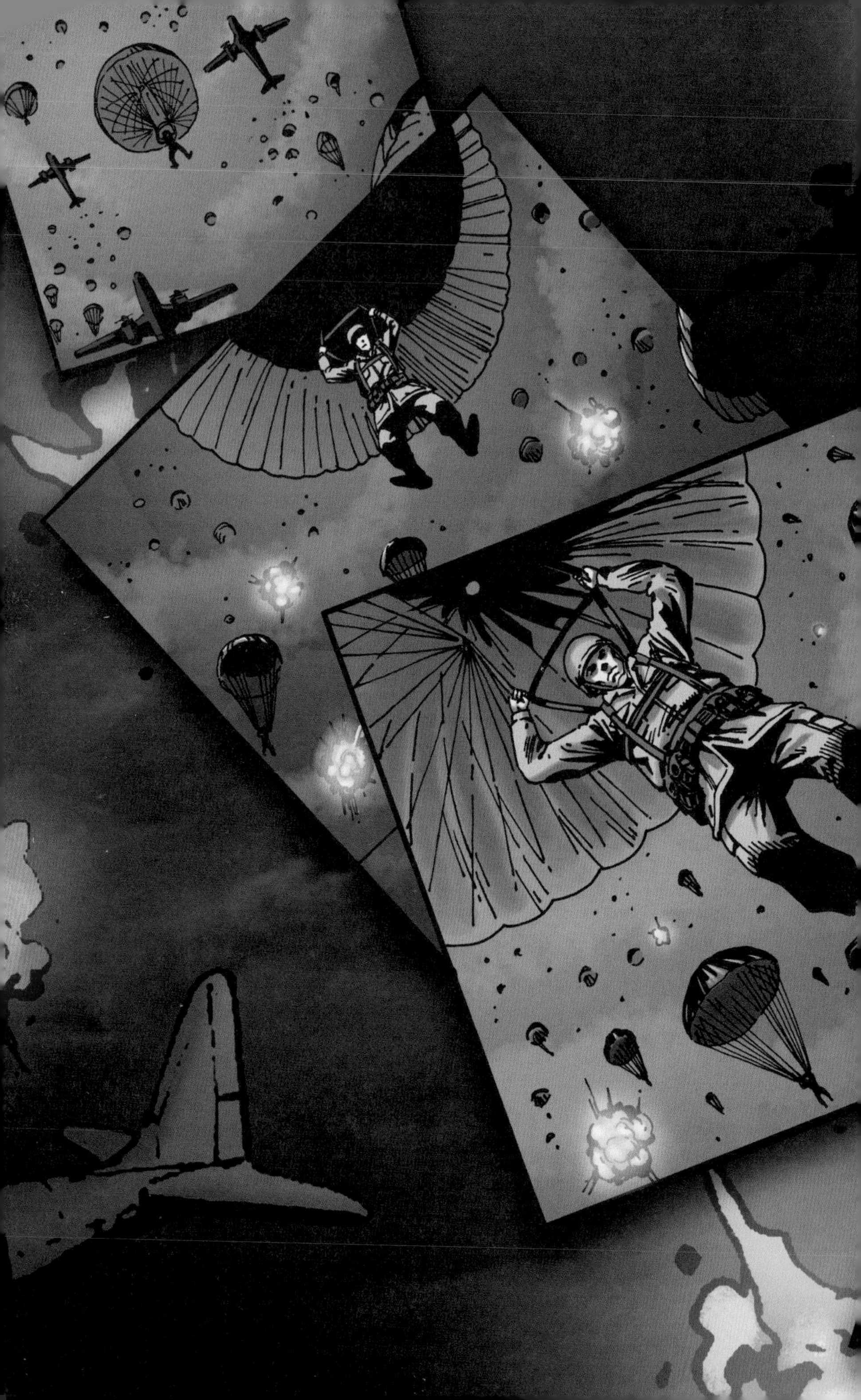

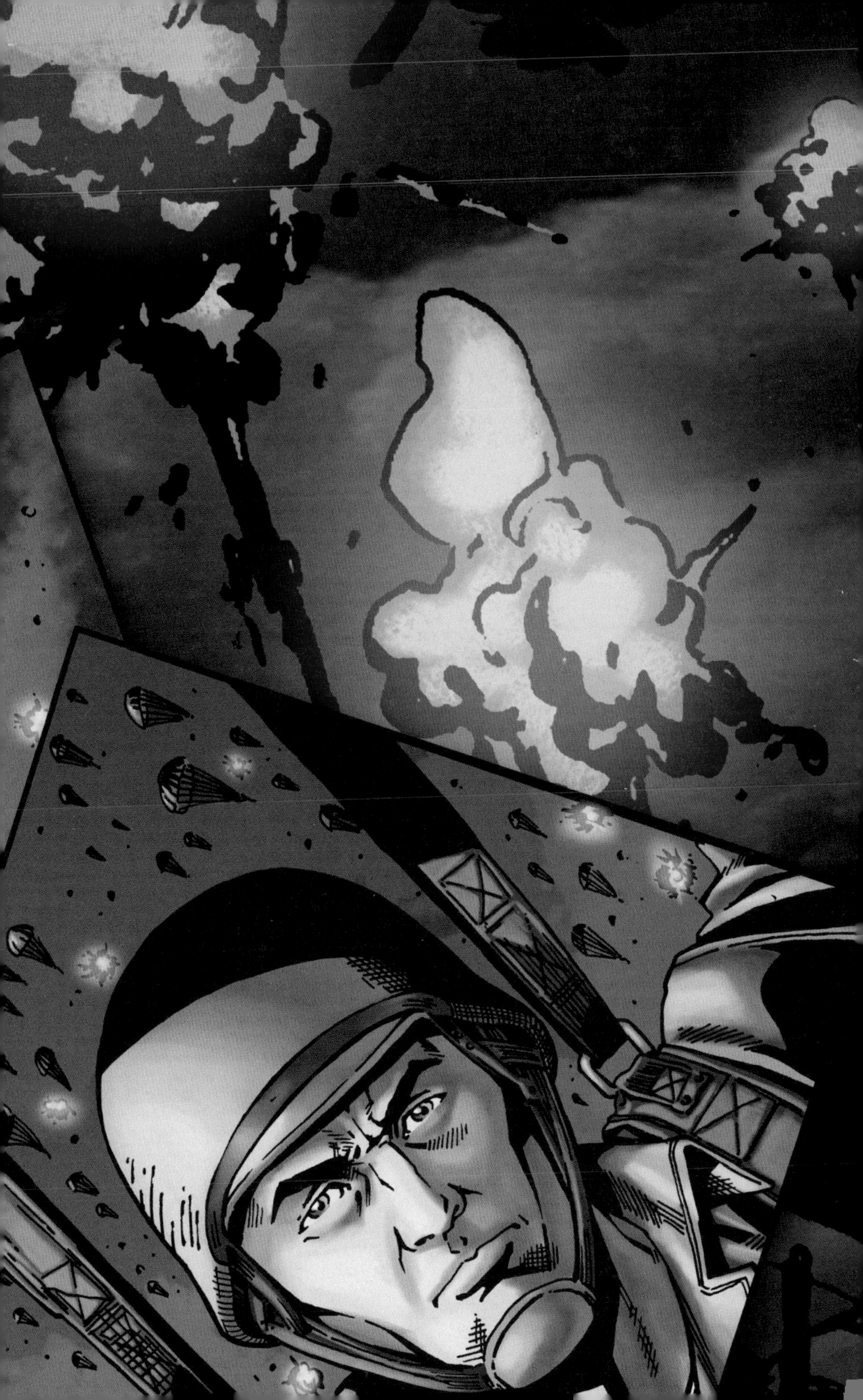

Private Donovan grasped the straps above his head. He finally caught a glimpse of his surroundings. Filled with parachutes, the sky looked like an invasion of green jellyfish floating toward the ground.

Donovan looked up.

An anti-aircraft shell hit his carrier plane. Shattering in a massive ball of flames, the remains of the C-47 erupted in front of his eyes.

But what about the pilot —? Donovan thought.

A moment later, red-hot wreckage whooshed past the newbie private. It nearly clipped his chute and blew him off course.

Seconds later, the ground rushed up to meet him. Knees bent, Donovan hit the soil with a thud, rolled, and came up ready to fight. Problem was, his equipment bag was missing. He didn't even have a weapon.

Suddenly, Private Donovan heard noises coming from the woods behind him. He quickly curled the parachute cords and silky canopy into a ball. Then he moved for the cover of some nearby trees.

No more than fifteen yards in front of him, a German patrol of ten soldiers marched toward his last position. Even in the frost-filled night, sweat formed on Donovan's head as the Nazi troops passed by. They scanned the area with their weapons drawn.

Fear gripped the young private. He could feel his heart about to burst through his chest. Quietly, Donovan crouched and leaned against a tree. His eyes darted for a way out.

Never had he been this scared. His hands shook like the leaves above his head. Should he move? Should he stay? If there was one patrol, more would follow. Without a weapon, he was as good as dead.

Donovan had to move. He waited for the German soldiers to pass. Then, as quietly as he could, he put one foot in front of the other. He crouched slowly in the dense underbrush. The air was so hushed, the breaking of one twig could alert the enemy.

Moments felt like days, but slowly Donovan gained distance on the German patrol. Finally, after more than an hour, he broke out of his crouch-walk and into a sprint. Where he was going, he had no idea. For now, he'd run as far from the Germans as he could.

Tears flowed down Donovan's cheeks as he ran. He cursed himself. *Coward!* But what could he do? He didn't have a rifle, a bayonet, or even a canteen. Was he going to fight off ten of Hitler's men with his helmet?

Stopping at the edge of a clearing, Private Donovan saw a small farmhouse in the distance. The windows were boarded, and no lights were on. The shelter looked abandoned. Glancing back to where the Nazis had been, he thought for a moment. Until he felt safe enough to move toward his platoon, this place would have to do.

DEBRIEFING

C-47 SKYTRAIN MILITARY TRANSPORT

SPECIFICATIONS

FIRST FLIGHT: 12-23-1941
WING SPAN: 95 feet 6 inches
LENGTH: 63 feet 9 inches
HEIGHT: 17 feet
WEIGHT: 31,000 pounds
CRUISE SPEED: 160 miles per hour
MAX RANGE: 3,600 miles
ACCOMMODATION: 3 crew and
6,000 pounds of cargo, or 28
airborne troops, or 14 stretcher
patients with 3 attendants.

FACT

During World War II, the Douglas
C-47 Skytrain became known by
soldiers as the "Gooney Bird."

HISTORY

In 1941, the Douglas Aircraft
Company modified a version of
their DC-3 airliner for military
use. The C-47 Skytrain became an
essential carrier aircraft during
World War II. By the end of the
war, more than 10,000 had been
built. Some carried equipment,
including fully-assembled Jeeps,
37-mm cannons, and medical
supplies. Others carried soldiers
with full combat gear into battle
or returned with wounded vets.
One version of the aircraft, known
as the C-53 Skytroop, dropped U.S.
paratroopers behind enemy lines.

U.S. PARATROOPERS

DROP ZONE

On August 13, 1940, at Lawson Field in Georgia, Lieutenant William T. Ryder made the first ever U.S. paratroop jump. By 1944, more than 13,000 paratroopers took to the skies during World War II. These men were part of Operation Overlord, an extensive military campaign aimed at stopping Nazi Germany. Although they planned to drop behind enemy lines, many were killed in the air or scattered across the dangerous countryside. More than 1,000 paratroopers died during the campaign and twice as many were injured.

FLAK

During World War II, the German army's anti-aircraft fire destroyed hundreds of U.S. aircraft and killed thousands of soldiers. These violent midair explosions are also known as flak.

CHAPTER 002
ISOLATION

Private Mike Donovan moved quickly but quietly. He feared more German soldiers might be lurking in the surrounding forests. While his eyes scanned, the private could feel a strong pressure in his head from the adrenaline pumping through his veins. He was tired and scared. The instinct to stay alive was the only thing keeping him going.

Night in France wasn't like night in Willow Creek, Illinois, where Donovan grew up. It wasn't even like Georgia, where he had trained for the invasion. No, this was a pitch-black night with few stars and no moon — an alien planet, for all he knew.

Donovan moved quietly through the dense underbrush toward the deserted home. The locks on the front door were rusted out. Dust was inches thick on the porch. That suited the rookie soldier just fine.

Stepping inside, Donovan fumbled in his left cargo pocket a bit. Finally, he lit the one piece of gear that seemed had survived the jump — his flashlight. The beam of light cut the darkness as he entered and scanned the deserted room.

Deserted was right.

No comforts here, only broken remains of wooden furniture. A few small chairs and a small table sat in the front room. The stairs leading to the second floor were smashed and littered with holes.

Private Donovan closed the door. He jammed a small scrap of plywood between the interior door handle and the frame. It wasn't a permanent fix, but he hoped to stop anyone who might want to come in.

The young private sat down at the dusty table. He removed his helmet and placed it on the table next to his flashlight. The floor below him creaked as his weight stressed the old wooden planks. Looking around, he knew this place was no safe haven.

But what next? Donovan wondered.

He looked at his watch. It had only been two hours since he leaped from the plane and landed in enemy territory. Daylight wouldn't come for a few more. Donovan didn't dare use the flashlight any more for fear the enemy would see it and zero in on him.

Rest and calm down, that's what I need to do, Donovan told himself. *You're alive. For now . . .*

The young private ran a shaking hand over his sweaty crew cut, trying to figure out his next move. The platoon didn't have a backup plan in case everyone got separated. His map case was gone. But from the direction of gunshots, he knew war was only a few miles away.

If he headed north, Donovan would, more than likely, meet up with other members of his platoon. But move during the daytime? Was that wise? Was it any safer than moving through occupied France at night, where the Germans had a home-field advantage?

His mind raced for a solution. But soon, his eyelids drooped, and PFC Michael Donovan — paratrooper from Dog Company, 2nd Battalion, 506th Parachute Infantry Regiment, 101st Airborne, 2nd Platoon — fell asleep.

CREEAAK!

In a heart-stopping fright, Donovan's eyes popped open. It was the sound of creaking wood from outside that had awakened him.

Like a shot, he was up, grabbing his helmet and looking around. Unknown by him, his flashlight had fallen off the table, hit the ground, and rolled out of his line of sight.

Through the spaces in the planks that covered the windows, he could see the shadows of men moving. The sun cut their forms into silhouettes.

Oh no, the sun! he thought. *How long have I been out?*

Quickly, Donovan looked around and assessed the situation. Nowhere to run, nowhere to hide. The house was empty with not even a sheet to cover the table and hide under. His eyes glanced toward the second floor.

CREEEEAKK! The wooden creaks from outside were louder again. They were closer to the front door. Like it or not, he knew the enemy would be coming in.

Maybe they're Americans, he thought. *Lost, scared, just like me.*

The private knew he could shout the verbal signal, "Flash," to which the proper Allied response was "Thunder." However, if they were German soldiers, he'd be giving himself away and killed instantly. Looking at the stairs again, Donovan knew he had to chance it.

As quietly as he could, Donovan moved and began to climb. One foot at a time, he did his best to step as lightly as possible. The wood was badly rotted. An unsteady footfall would shatter them, sending him crashing to the ground and alerting his visitors.

The soldiers were at the door, rattling the handle. Almost to the top now, excitement got the better of Donovan. He slipped. His left foot fell into a hole between the second stair from the top. Desperately, the private tried to free himself. Then he heard the voices.

"Es ist fest und wird nicht sich öffnen!" said a man.

Donovan couldn't understand the language, but he knew what it was.

German.

"Brechen sie es dann unten!" another yelled.

WHUMP! WHUMP! The sound of a shoulder hitting wood boomed into the small, empty house. Donovan pulled with all his might, but could not free his foot from the stairs.

He had only seconds as, over and over again, the shoulder hit. The pounding echoed all around him. Donovan pulled, twisted, and yanked, but nothing he did would free his foot.

Finally, just as the door came crashing open, the wooden stair splintered, and Donovan quickly dove around the banister. Peering down through the small holes in the wooden ceiling, the young private could see the first floor.

Nazi soldiers, three of them armed to the teeth, entered the building.

They stood for a moment, guns scanning. After a long beat, they entered farther. One room at a time, they split up and secured the first floor.

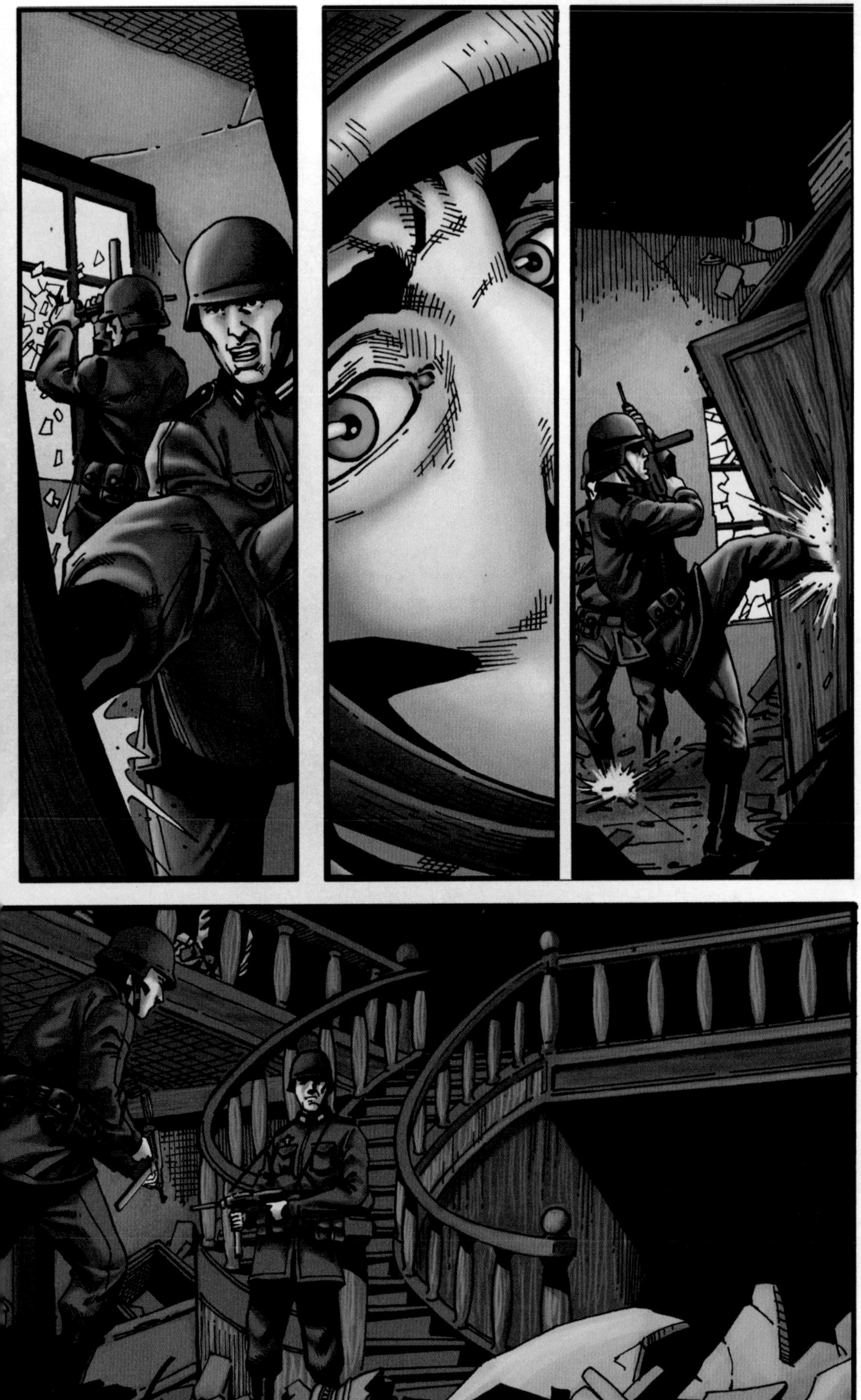

Finally, deciding the house was empty, two of the Nazis removed their helmets. They entered the small living room where the table and chairs sat.

Just then, one of the Nazi soldiers stopped and nodded at the stairs.

His friend smiled back, pointed to the rotting wood, and shrugged. The stairs were in such bad shape, he obviously figured there was no way anyone could be up there.

Grinning, he peered upward.

With a pull of the trigger, the soldier blasted ammo randomly through the ceiling.

Tightening the grip on his legs, Donovan curled himself into a small ball. The bullets ripped up through the floor all around him. He wanted to scream — to yell out — but he didn't.

"Wenn es jedermann oben dort gibt, ist er jetzt tot!" the German said.

He laughed and continued spraying bullets into the ceiling.

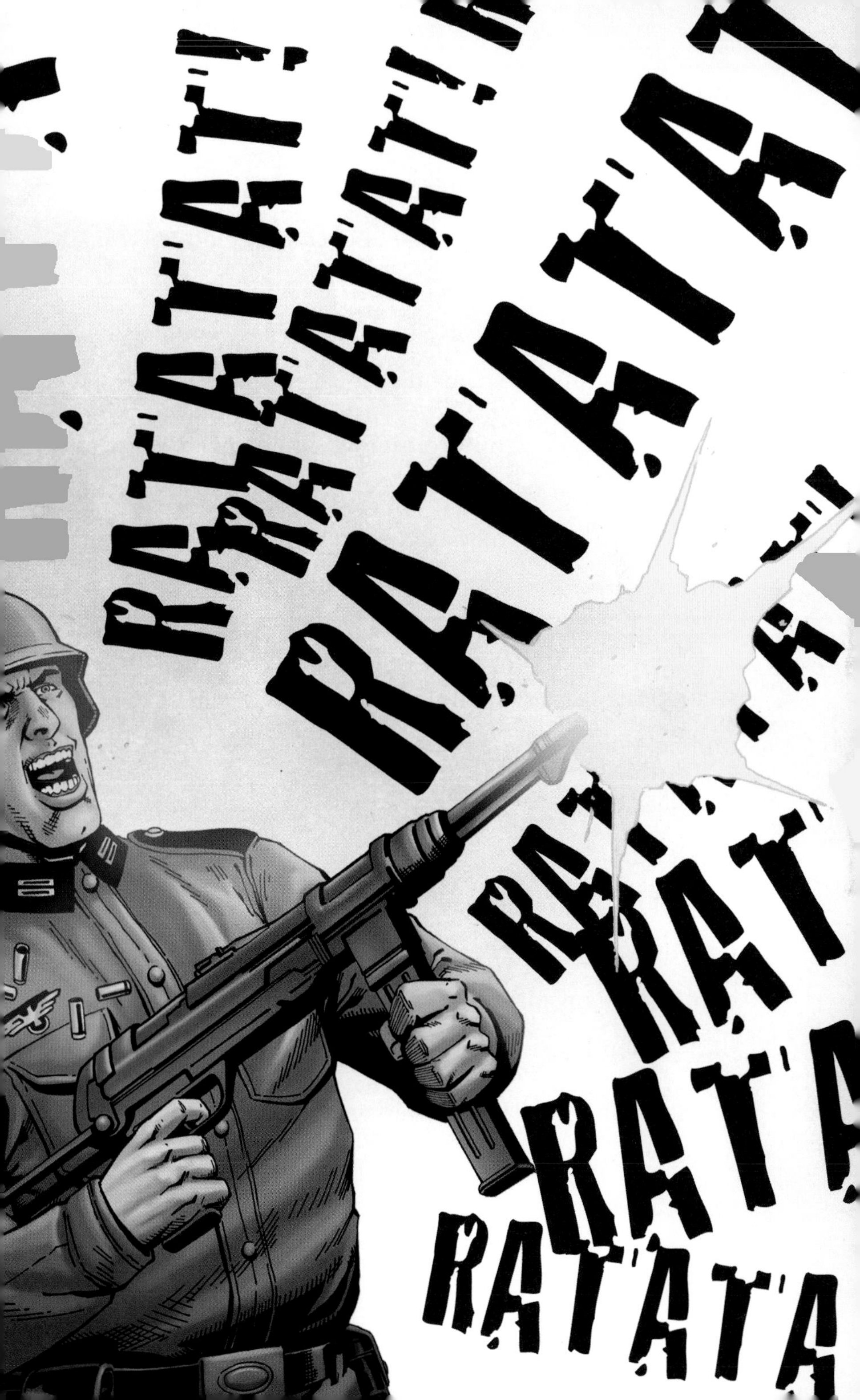
RATATATATA!
RATATATATA!
RATATATA
RATATA
RATA
RATA
RATATA

The shooter shouldered his weapon, took out a pack of cigarettes, and offered one to each of the others. All three of them lit up. *Hopefully,* Donovan thought, *they won't look up at their smoke trails.* The Nazis would see him clear as day through the holes in the ceiling.

Time passed. Minutes turned to hours as the Germans sat and enjoyed their time away from the war. They were calm and relaxed, taking an unauthorized break from patrolling the woods.

Not Donovan. He was a bundle of nerves. At any second, the Germans might look up, notice his shape, and he'd be dead.

His legs began cramping from being balled up. He didn't dare shift. Even the slightest movement could cause the ceiling to creak, drawing the enemy's gaze upward. If he didn't move, didn't make a sound, and as long as they didn't come upstairs, he'd be safe. Or so he thought. And that's when he saw it.

His flashlight. The army-issued flashlight was still under the table. It was only a matter of time before the Germans spotted it and began searching for him.

Donovan's pulse quickened. His hands began to shake again. The young private's eyes darted from side to side, looking for a way out. But there was nothing he could do. If he as much as breathed heavily, he'd be discovered.

Private Donovan watched as the shooter bent down to tighten his boot lace and froze. Squinting, the Nazi didn't recognize it at first. As he slowly reached out and picked up the flashlight, he knew exactly what it was. Eyes wide, the German soldier sat up and looked at his friends.

"*Amerikaner . . .*" he said as he turned to the flashlight. "*Amerikaner!!*"

Quickly, the Germans' guns came up, and they went on alert. Donovan's world exploded in a hail of bullets that pierced the farmhouse and shattered the wood.

TATAT! RATATAT! RATA

But these shots weren't aimed at him. These shots came from outside.

Huddled in a ball, Donovan screamed as hot lead splintered the flooring around him.

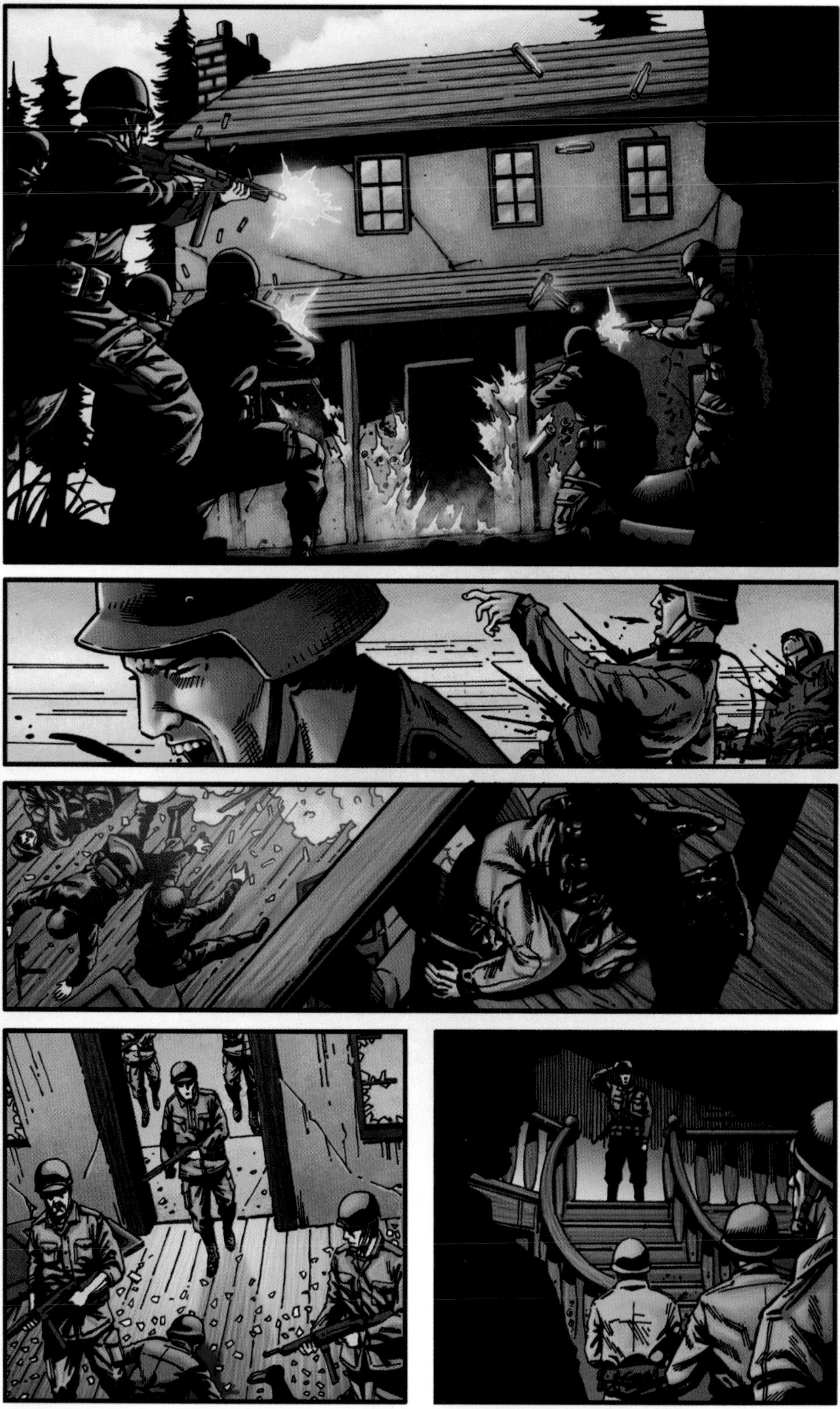

All at once, the German soldiers were racked with rounds, fell to the ground, and stopped breathing.

"Flash!" someone yelled from outside.

Donovan looked down from his perch. He was shocked to be alive and to hear an American voice.

"Thunder! Thunder!" the private yelled back.

Creeping down the stairs, Donovan looked as PFC Peretti and Sergeant Anness of Dog Company popped their heads around the door frame.

"Sarge?!" Donovan yelled.

Eyes wide, Anness came in the doorway. "Donovan!"

The men shook hands.

"What the heck happened to you?" asked Anness.

"Yeah, how'd you end up here?" Peretti added. He watched Donovan reach down and retrieve his flashlight from the floor.

"I was, uh —" Donovan began. "When the plane exploded, I was blown off course. I missed the Drop Zone." He didn't dare tell them of his incredible fear.

"Really? I thought we were supposed to drop into a farmhouse full of Germans," Private Peretti joked. He laughed as Anness jabbed him in the side, sensing Donovan's anxiety.

"Don't worry, kid. It's okay," said Sergeant Anness.

Donovan continued, "I lost my musette bag, my map, my rifle, everything. After I hit the ground last night, I saw this place, and thought I'd wait until someone found me."

"Yeah, half the entire invasion force is scattered across France," Sergeant Anness explained. "Lieutenant Spears ordered us to recon the area to look for 'em. Glad we found you!" The sergeant reached down and took one of the German's MP40 machine guns. He handed it to Donovan. "You'll need this," he said.

Donovan looked up. "We, uh, lose anyone?"

Peretti's eyes quickly saddened. "Yeah," he said after a moment. "Lots."

Donovan nodded and flipped off the safety on the MP40. "Where are we going now?" he asked.

"Listen . . ." Sergeant Anness replied with a smile.
He pointed toward the sound of cannon fire in the
distance.

"That-a-way," he said.

MP40 MACHINE GUN

SPECIFICATIONS

FIRST USED: 1939
MANUFACTURER: Erma Werke
TYPE: Submachine gun
LENGTH: 32.8 inches
WEIGHT: 8.82 pounds
RANGE: 328 feet
NUMBER BUILT: 1 million
RATE OF FIRE: 500/minute

FACT

Allied forces nicknamed the MP40 the "Schmeisser," after weapons designer Hugo Schmeisser. However, Schmeisser created the MP18, not the MP40 machine gun.

HISTORY

During World War II, Germany developed the MP40, which stood for *Maschinenpistole*, or Machine Pistol. Designed by Heinrich Vollmer, this lightweight submachine gun quickly became a Nazi-killing machine. The fully automatic, open-bolt design enabled the gun to discharge 550 rounds per minute. Even in the 1940s, this rate of fire was fairly slow. However, the decrease in speed allowed for increased accuracy when firing single shots – an advantage in the short-range, urban-combat situations of European cities.

NAZI GERMANY

HISTORY

The Nazi Party, or National Socialist German Workers' Party, ruled Germany from 1933 to 1945. It was led by Adolf Hitler, a feared dictator who sought to expand Germany's influence around the globe and "cleanse" the world of all "inferior" races. For a time, he succeeded. After invading Poland in 1939, Germany expanded its control across most of Europe and Northern Africa through a series of violent military campaigns. They also killed millions of Jews and other minorities during the genocide known as the Holocaust.

THE HOLOCAUST

Before they were stopped in 1945, the Nazis began their most vicious campaign known as the Final Solution, or the Holocaust. During this period, Jews, homosexuals, Jehovah's Witnesses, Polish Catholics, disabled people, and other minorities were captured by Nazi soldiers and forced into brutal confines called concentration camps. There, victims were often given inhumane tasks and more than 6 million of them were killed. After the war, many German leaders were convicted of these horrific war crimes.

CHAPTER 003

COURAGE

The rally point wasn't as far as Private Donovan thought it would be. The trek ended up only being a bit over five miles to the northeast. If he had mustered the courage to move last night, Donovan could have regrouped with his platoon in under an hour. But from the sounds of the weapons firing in the distance, he had thought it to be much farther away. At least that's how he justified the fear to himself.

Sergeant Anness and Private Peretti had gone this way before. They had rescued other lost paratroops and had the route memorized. Thousands of men had been blown off course, and to the luck of the Allies, this complete failure had turned into a major advantage.

"Caught the Nazis totally off guard with the drops," Peretti explained to Donovan. "The best part? We completely disrupted all of the German outposts."

"With a million of us running around like crazy," Peretti continued. "The Germans don't know where to shoot! Confusion helped us get some tanks and heavy equipment up onto the beaches, but our reinforcements are —"

RUUSSSSTLE

Movement in the nearby trees made him go quiet.

Holding up a closed fist, Private Peretti silently ordered the men to stop. Opening a hand, he waved his palm toward the ground. He signaled all three soldiers to go into a crouch.

Private Donovan looked at his own hand. It began shaking again. He made a tight fist, trying to stop it. He couldn't.

The rustling was getting closer.

"Flash!" shouted Peretti. No response came back.

"FLASH!" he shouted again.

Nearby, Sergeant Anness raised his Thompson machine gun to his shoulder, ready to fire.

Just then, a muffled "Thunder!" came out of the forest in front of them.

Standing, the trio was pleasantly surprised to see Private "Popeye" Wynne and Private Gordon emerge from the trees. Both men were from Easy Company.

Sergeant Anness smiled. "Look what we found," he said, pointing at Donovan.

"Nice to see ya, kid," said Popeye. "We're over here."

*　*　*

The road to the town of Angoville-Au-Plain changed quickly from a deserted tree-lined path to a village buzzing with American activity. Soldiers and troopers from every company, Easy to Dog, and most of the entire 2nd Battalion had assembled here in the town square.

As they walked in, Donovan noticed groups of soldiers on the grassy berms. They laughed, ate chow, and milled around like they were on vacation.

All of this felt wrong.

Nothing had gone right since wheels-up in England. Donovan wasn't sure if it ever really would. Everything was a failure. The plan, the insertion, the drop. *Heck,* he thought, looking down at his shaking hand. *I'm carrying a German machine gun, for Pete's sake.* Had none of them been through what he had? Had none of them been as scared as he had been?

Donovan asked himself these questions as he regrouped with the other members of his platoon at the company assembly area and checked in with his platoon sergeant. They were excited to see him alive. Even though they invited him to relax with them as they ate, Donovan felt strangely detached from his friends. He slowly shuffled away from the others, alone. He felt like they were all looking at him, like they knew he had hidden in that farmhouse to get away from the war.

Donovan fought back the tears as his mind drifted away from France, away from the war, and back to home. Walking off by himself, he reached into his left jacket pocket and pulled out a piece of paper. He unfolded the dirty, worn envelope. It was a well-read letter from his fiancee, Renee.

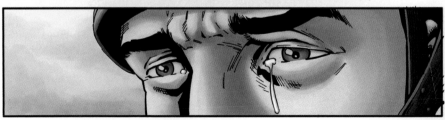

I love you

Slumping onto the ground, the tears came freely as he wept. Donovan wondered if he was ever going to get home to see her. He clasped a hand over his mouth, trying to keep quiet when he heard someone approach.

"Can I sit?" said a voice from behind.

Donovan looked up to see Sergeant Anness coming out of the shadows and into the light. The sergeant had a duffle bag slung over his shoulder. Donovan nodded a silent "yes" as the Sergeant sat next to him.

"I know what you did, Private," Anness said, reaching into the bag. "And I know it's eating at you."

Donovan looked at him. "What do you —?" he said.

"Hiding in the farmhouse," Anness continued. "I jumped out right after you and saw where you landed. By the time I got to your position, you were gone. Soon after, I got picked up by members of Easy Company."

"I was so scared!" Donovan explained. "I was more scared than I ever was in my whole life, Sarge."

"I know, kid, and I'm not here to make you feel guilty," said Anness. "Heck, I might have done the same."

"I'm a coward," Donovan said through the tears.

Looking down at Donovan's hands, Anness saw the letter he held tightly. "You're not a coward," he said to the private. "You were trapped with three German soldiers and no weapon. You were scared, and I understand. We all do. But we're here now, on the front lines, and no amount of wishing or praying's going to change that."

"You need to reach deep down inside you," the sergeant continued. "Find that courage to carry on and hold on to it tight. That's the only way you're going to get back home — to make it through this alive."

Donovan nodded as the sergeant stood. "We're not here for the pay," added Anness. "And we're certainly not here for the chow."

Donovan chuckled through his tears.

"We're here for each other," said the sergeant. "We do what we have to do so the guy on the left and the guy on the right can go home again. They'd do the same for you, understood?"

"Yes, Sarge," Donovan replied.

"Good," said Anness. He offered a hand and helped Donovan up from the ground. "Then I need you."

After unslinging a gun from his shoulder, Anness handed it over to Donovan. Then he gave him a bandoleer full of ammo magazines.

"Easy Company's been tasked to take out four German 88 anti-aircraft guns that're pounding the beaches," said the sergeant. "Lieutenant Spears wants us to assist with an ammo drop. You'll be with me on the heavy as my backup along the tree line. Weapons and ammo only. Leave everything else."

Donovan nodded. He slapped a magazine into the receiver, racked the action, and readied the gun to fire with a loud clack.

CLAK!

The sound jolted Donovan's nerves a bit. "Okay," said the young private.

Nearby, Anness loaded his M1 Garand rifle. "Then let's move out," commanded the sergeant.

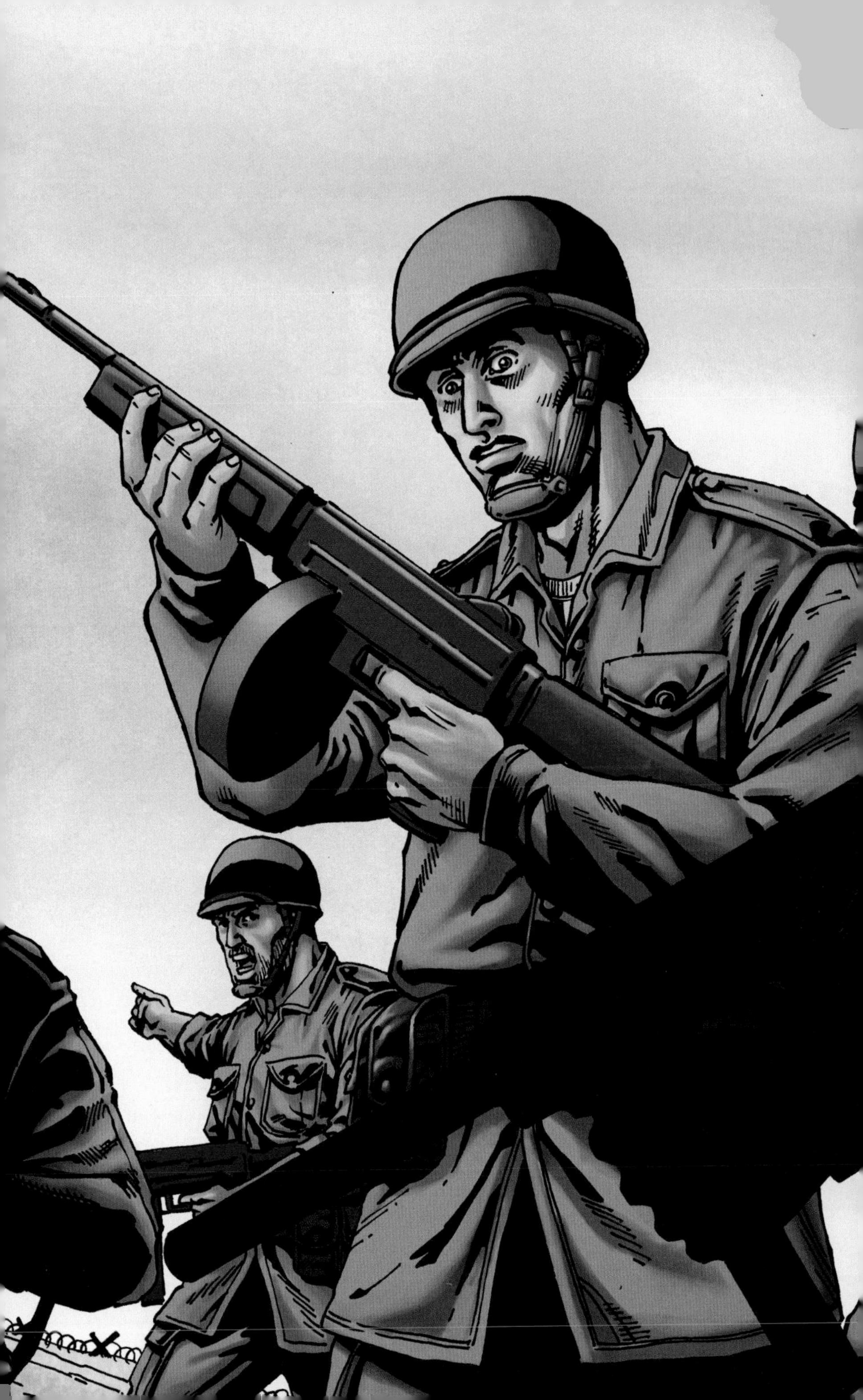

EASY COMPANY

SPECIFICATIONS

MILITARY BRANCH: U.S. Army
ACTIVE: 1942-1945
TYPE: Infantry
ROLE: Airborne
SIZE: 139 soldiers
NICKNAME: Screaming Eagles
MOTTO: "Currahee"
BATTLES: Battle of Normandy;
Battle of Carentan; Operation
Market Garden; Battle of the Bulge

HISTORY

Created in 1942 as part of the 506th Parachute Infantry Regiment of the U.S. Army, Easy Company played a critical role during WWII. On June 6, 1944, as part of Operation Overlord, these paratroops were dropped over Normandy, France, from C-47 transport aircrafts. Many soldiers missed their targets and were scattered across enemy territory. However, after regrouping, the men of Easy Company fulfilled their mission by disabling several German batteries and supporting troops already on the ground.

FACT

In 2001, Easy Company was featured in the HBO Emmy-winning miniseries *Band of Brothers*.

GERMAN 88

HISTORY

Although developed before the Spanish Civil War (1936-1939), the German 88 anti-aircraft gun was most effective during WWII. Nazi soldiers could use these high-powered weapons to shoot down Allied aircraft at an altitude of nearly 30,000 feet. However, the German 88 proved most useful as an anti-tank artillery gun. When attached to a mobile mount, the gun could seek out enemy tanks. Firing highly explosive 20-pound shells, the German 88 could pierce the armor of any tank and reload at a rate of 15 to 20 rounds a minute.

M1 Garand

Developed by John C. Garand, the M1 rifle was adopted by the U.S. Army in 1936. It was the first semi-automatic rifle used by soldiers and quickly became the most popular.

CHAPTER 004

GET UP AND FIRE

The trees seem much prettier, greener, in the daytime, Donovan thought. The young private moved through the forest with the eight other members of Dog Company. Standing in the center of a tactical column formation, he tried desperately to keep his fear in check. He concentrated on anything other than the sounds of thunder coming from in front of them.

But it didn't help. Every snapping branch or rustling leaf made his heart jump and head swivel.

The explosions and firing got louder as the men approached a clearing. The opening was about forty yards square, surrounded by a line of tall trees. At the far end, three of the four howitzer cannons were placed so they could angle in on the beach for German fire support. The fourth and final cannon was set back at a ninety-degree angle from the first.

KABLAMO!

Through the trees, Donovan watched the third 88 explode as members of Easy Company ran through the trenches that connected the massive cannons. Germans flooded the area with bullets from the tree lines and the far end of the trenches. They were trying anything and everything to halt the American attack.

Lieutenant Spears stopped and raised a hand. Like a third base coach, he silently signaled his men what to do.

On his command, they split up. He and five others went toward the third cannon where Easy Company was pinned down. Donovan and Anness moved left, behind the cover of a small berm.

Once in position, Sergeant Anness pulled up a heavy machine gun and placed its tripod on the grass. Handing him a belt of ammo, Donovan got ready to load the Browning M1919 medium machine gun. Then suddenly, hot lead whizzed by their ears.

RATATAT! RATATAT!

Bullets chipped and splintered the trees. They embedded themselves in the thick, French dirt right in front of the Americans. Twenty German soldiers, only forty yards away, began firing everything from MG42s to MP40s over the area.

They ducked as Anness yelled to Donovan, "Get that belt in there!"

Donovan jammed the ammo belt into the machine gun. The gun's holding bar at the entrance of the feedway grabbed and held it in place. Ratcheting the handle, Donovan nervously looked over at Anness.

"Go!" shouted the sergeant.

The machine gun sprang to life. It threw bullets at the enemy and spit empty brass shells to the ground. Across the knoll, Germans twisted and fell as the slugs struck their bodies.

At the same time, a German stick grenade soared through the air. It landed behind Anness and Donovan with a thud. They both stared at each other.

"Grenade!" shouted Sergeant Anness.

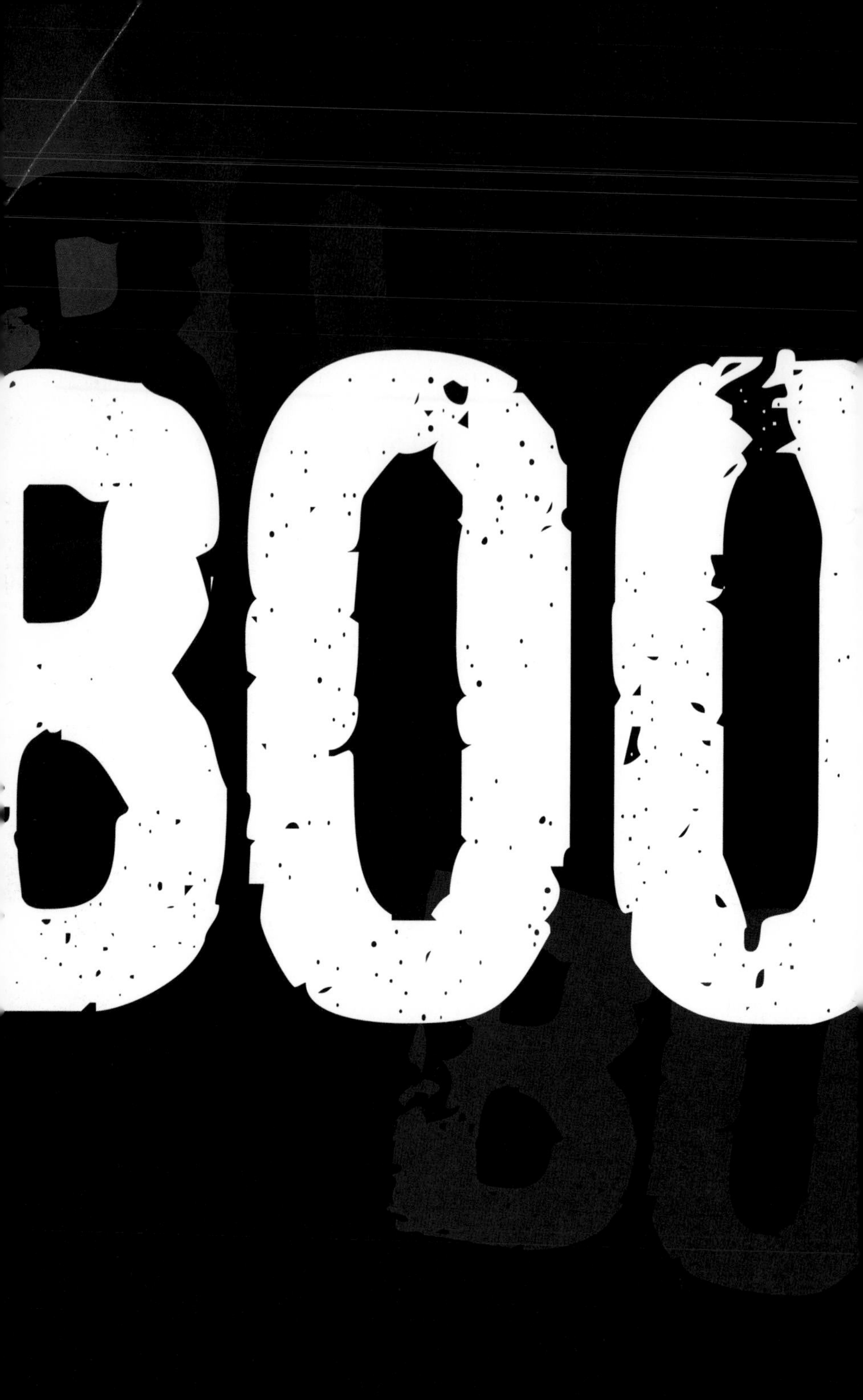
BOO

OM

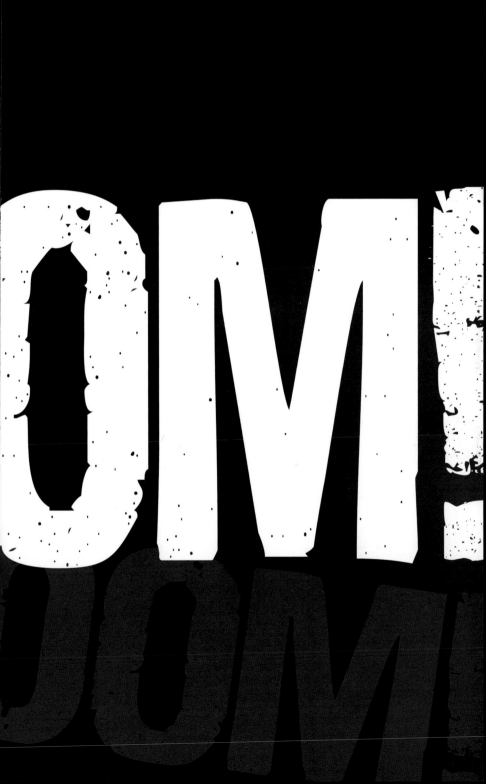

The grenade exploded, creating a massive crater in the ground and showering the pair with rocks and soil. Anness kept firing, but Donovan, shaken by the concussion, rolled and slipped into the hole. He covered his head and pulled on his helmet to protect his face.

Looking down at him, Anness was concerned. "What's wrong?!" he yelled. "Are you hit?"

Donovan didn't say a word. He just cowered in the hole, frozen with fear and crying.

"Are you hurt?!" Sergeant Anness asked again.

Donovan shook his head. "No! I'm just —"

"Then get up!" Anness shouted. "Come on! Get up!"

Slowly, Donovan looked up at Anness, who was standing, firing his machine gun and facing the enemy. He was powerful, optimistic, full of confidence. Eyeing his sergeant, Donovan wondered if he'd ever be that way.

The firing was so loud, so intense, that Donovan didn't know what to do. His heart pounded through his chest. He wanted to move, but his legs wouldn't let him.

"Fire your weapon!" yelled Anness. "Pour it on 'em!"

Finally, Donovan rose, his weapon clutched in his hands. Like a crutch, he leaned on it for support.

From a distance, he could see Lieutenant Spears slide in next to Lieutenant Winters, the chief officer of Easy Company. Handing off bags of ammo, Spears got a nod from Lieutenant Winters. Then, under the cover of fire support, Spears ran off. He was followed by the five other Dog Company soldiers sprinting down the trench line.

But suddenly, Spears did something unexpected. He got out of the cover of the trench, running along the top of it, followed by the five other soldiers. Three of them were killed instantly when the German's took their shots.

Five more German soldiers stood up from the cover of the tall grass in the field. They prepared to finish off Spears and the rest of the men.

Anness screamed, "Covering fire!"

Donovan could see the Germans bearing down on the U.S. troops. They had only seconds. That's when it happened. All around Donovan, the battle slowed. The butt of his rifle pushed tightly to his shoulder, Donovan took aim and put pressure on the trigger.

He fired.

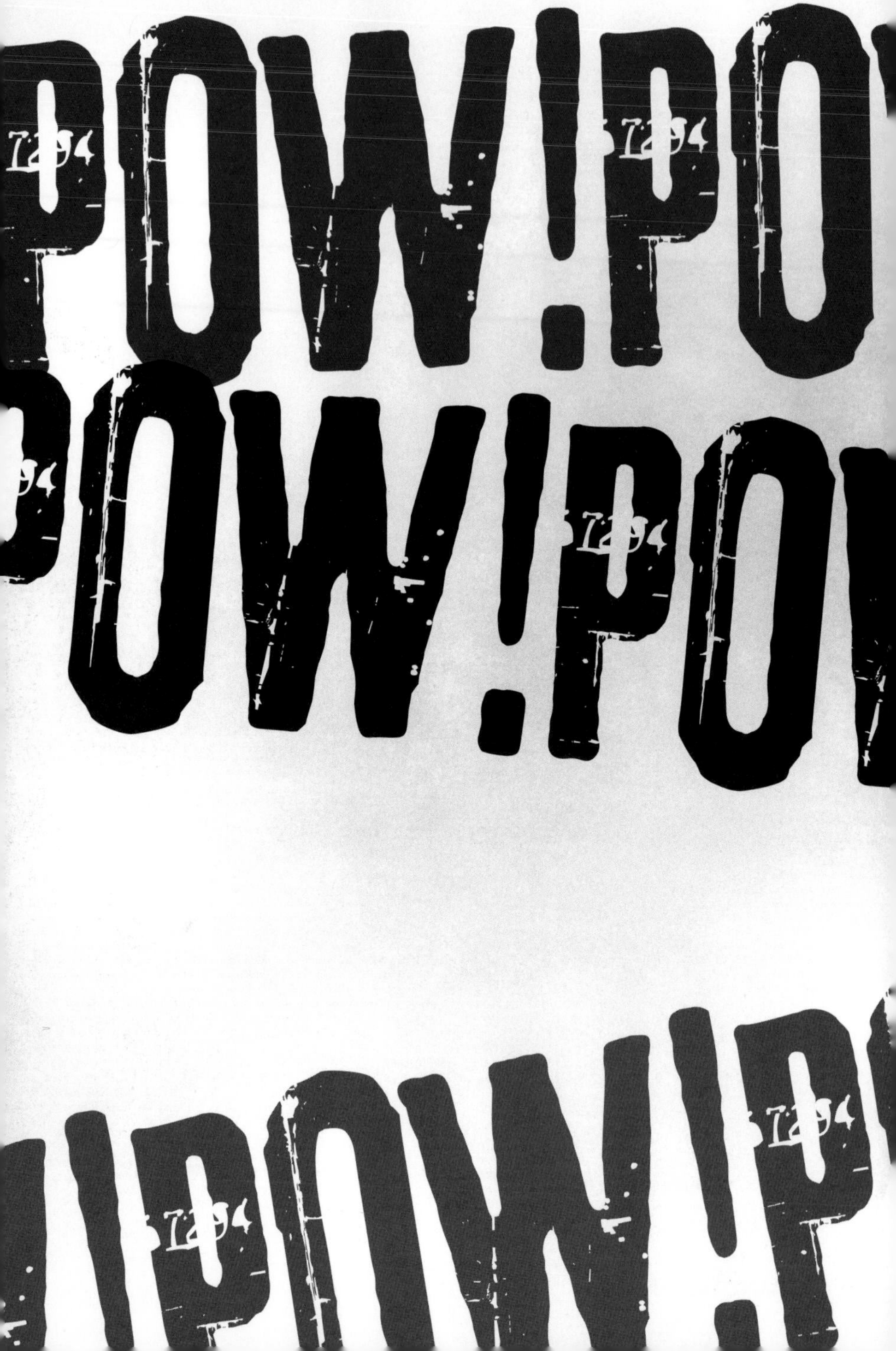
POW!PO
POW!POW
POW!P

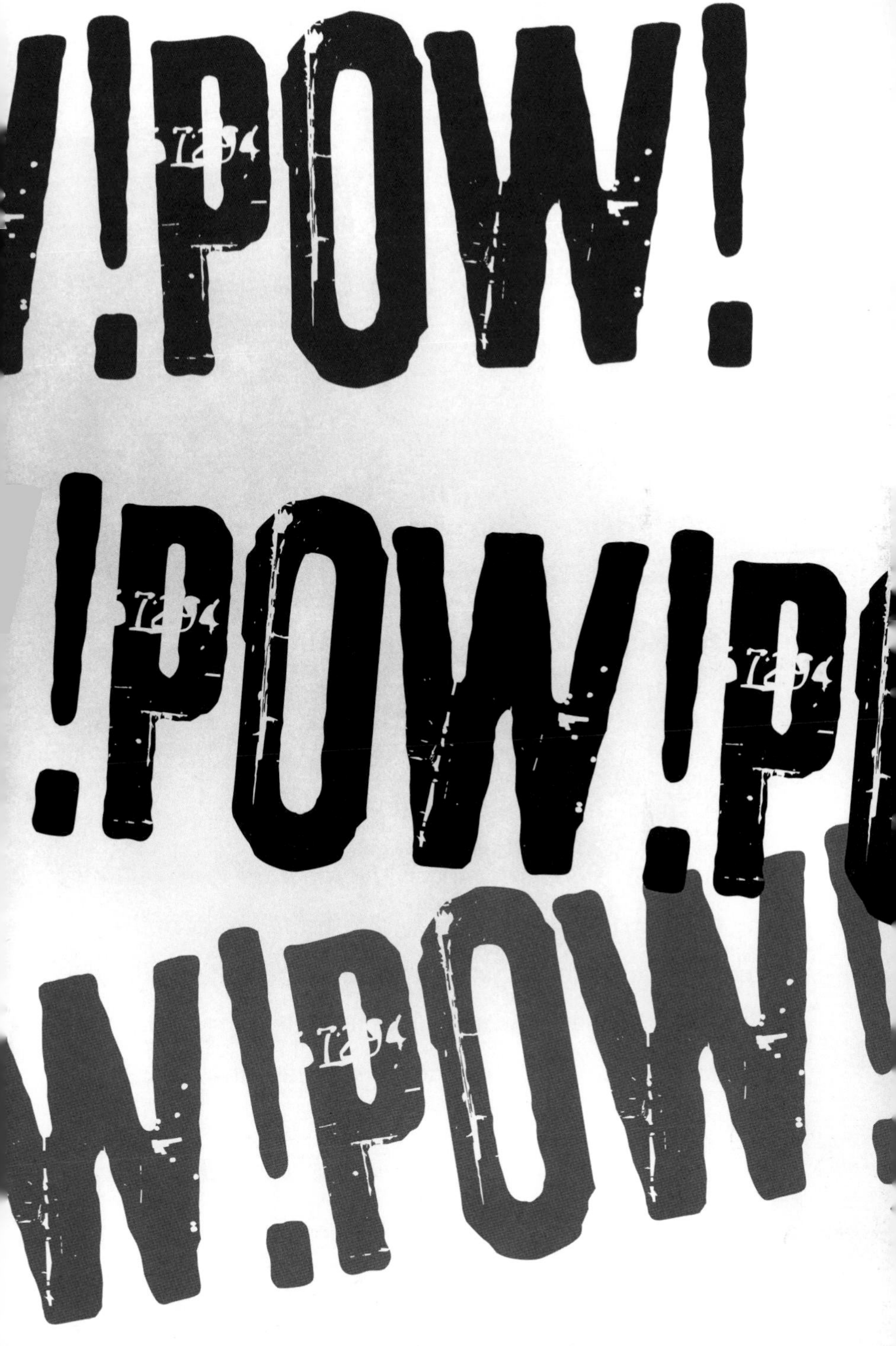
!POW!
!POW!
!POW!

Brass casings flipped out of his weapon as it discharged.

Fifty yards away, a Nazi's shoulder jerked. He twisted backward and fell to the ground.

Another squeeze, and it happened again. A second German dropped.

Anness grinned. "That's it, Donovan! Keep it —"

But his calls of inspiration were cut short as bullets racked Anness's body.

Donovan looked over just in time to watch his sergeant, his friend, collapse to the ground. Dead.

Ahead of him, the three remaining Germans had zeroed in on their position and were firing.

Instantly, Donovan was on the machine gun, pulling the trigger. His fury boiled over. With the power of the weapon fueling his emotions, he let out a yell from the bottom of his gut. A war cry like no other came from his lungs as he mowed down the three remaining German soldiers.

RATATAT! RATATAT

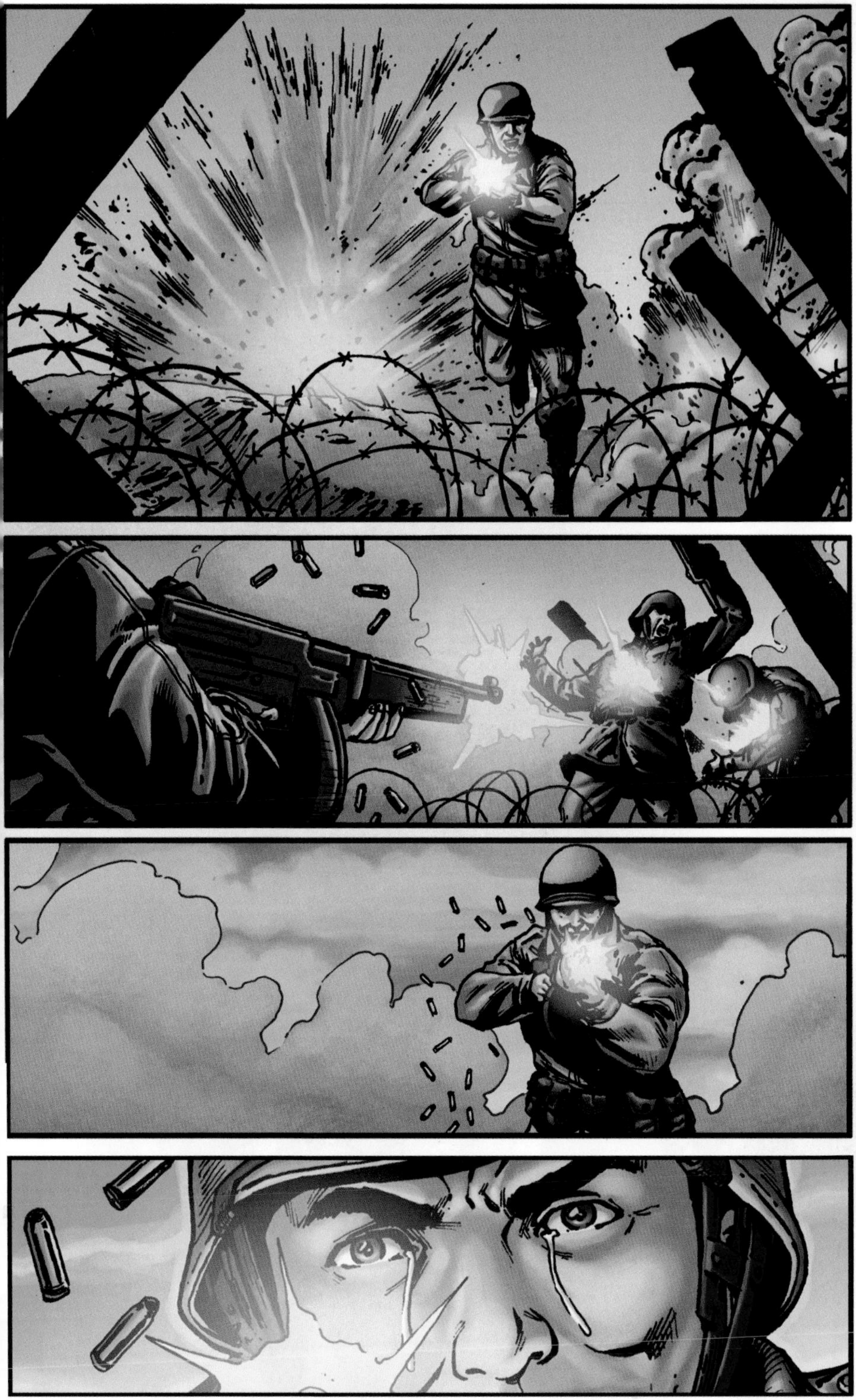

Dropping the machine gun, Donovan went to Sergeant Anness's side.

"Sarge?! Sarge!" he shouted.

Donovan put pressure on the wounds.

It was too late.

Anness was gone.

Overcome with emotions, Donovan began to cry again. He'd never lost a friend before, and he didn't know what to do. Looking down, his hands were covered in the sticky life-giving liquid that flowed from his friend's body. He noticed they were shaking, but this time it wasn't fear that made them tremble. It was anger.

A sudden explosion drew his attention.

The Americans' TNT blew the barrel of the last howitzer to shreds. Smoke poured out of it like a chimney. Then the shooting began to slow.

Private Donovan could hear Lieutenant Winters yelling, "Cease fire! Pull back to your original positions! Everyone back to battalion!"

And like that, the battle was over.

A crunch of leaves behind him made Donovan spin, his weapon held high.

"Whoa!" said Lieutenant Spears as he and Peretti raised their hands in the air.

Peretti's face sunk as he looked down and saw Anness's body. "Sarge," said the soldier.

"We'd better get him back," interrupted Spears. The Lieutenant and Peretti reached for the body, but Donovan stood, blocking their path.

"No," Donovan said, choking back his sobs. "I'll do it, sir."

Lieutenant Spears narrowed his eyes and shouldered his weapon. "You sure, Donovan?" he asked.

"I'll take care of him, sir," replied Donovan. "I owe him that much."

Bending over, the young private wiped away the dirt from Anness's lifeless face. Then he lifted him off the ground.

"Come on, Sarge," he whispered. "You're going home."

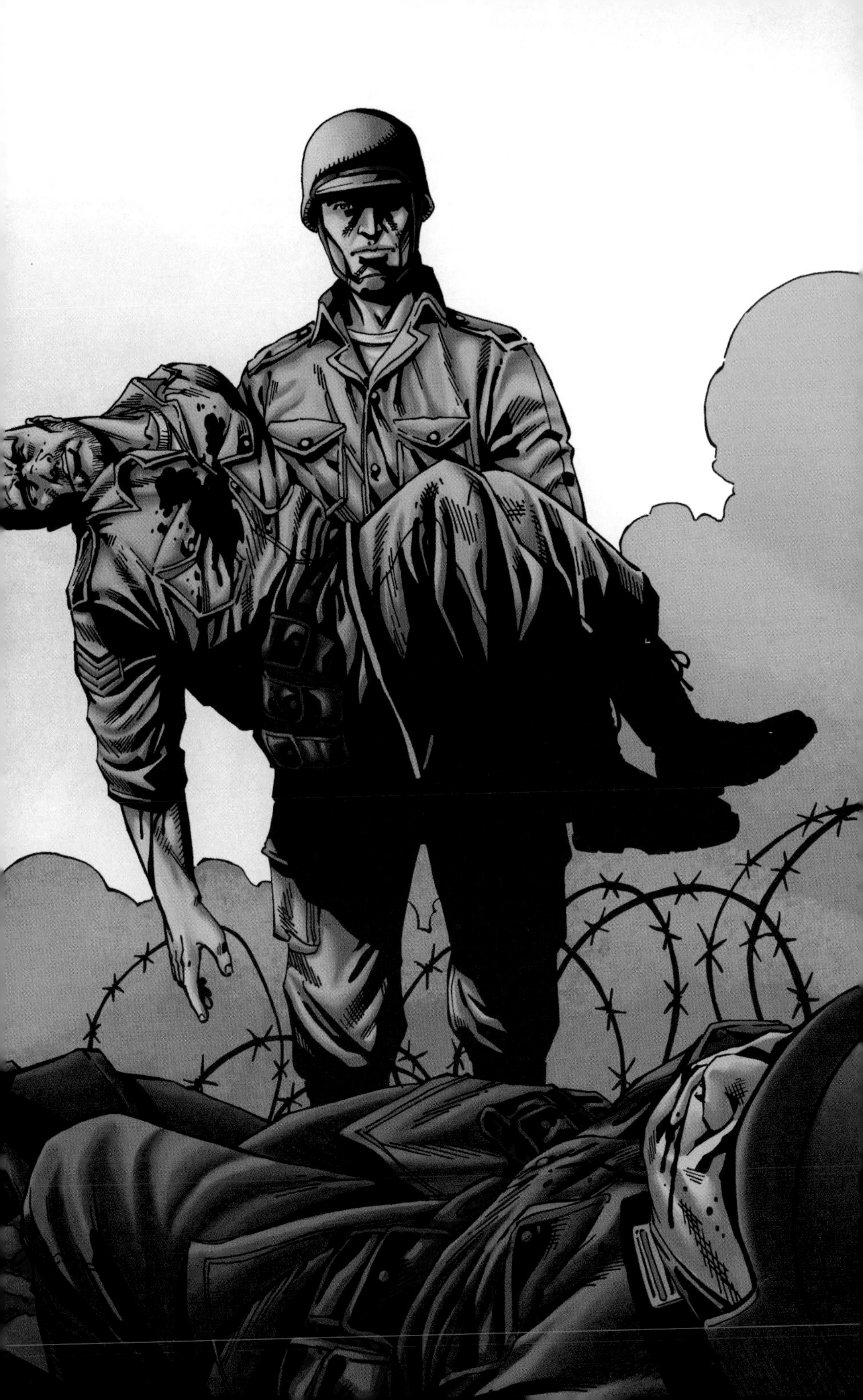

DEBRIEFING

CASUALTIES OF WORLD WAR II

HISTORY

With a total of more than 60 million casualties, World War II was the deadliest conflict in history. Many of these deaths were innocent civilians, including six million Jews and other minorities killed during the Holocaust. Some countries, including Lithuania and Poland, lost nearly 15 percent of their total population in the war.

STATISTICS

Nearly 60 countries suffered losses during WWII. Here are some of the gruesome totals:

COUNTRY	TOTAL DEATHS
China	10-20 million
Dutch East Indies	3-4 million
France	570,000
Germany	6-9 million
Japan	2.7 million
Poland	5.5-6 million
Soviet Union	24 million
United Kingdom	450,000
United States	420,000

FACT

Historians estimate that nearly 5 million prisoners of war died while still in captivity during WWII.

NORMANDY AMERICAN CEMETERY

HISTORY

The United States suffered heavy losses during WWII. The largest number of deaths came on July 6, 1944, during the invasion of Normandy, now known as D-Day. Today, 9,387 soldiers still rest on European soil at the American Cemetery and Memorial in Colleville-sur-Mer, Normandy, France. The 172-acre cemetery overlooks Omaha Beach, where U.S. troops stormed ashore during their D-Day assault. Of the deaths that day, 1,557 Americans were never located or identified. A memorial wall at the cemetery honors these unknown soldiers.

WWII MEMORIAL

On April 29, 2004, the National World War II Memorial opened in Washington, D.C. This site, located near the Washington Monument, honors the 16 million U.S. soldiers who served during WWII and the more than 400,000 who were killed. The memorial features 56 granite pillars, two 43-foot arches, a large fountain, and a reflecting pool. Operated by the National Park Service, the memorial has averaged more than 4.4 million visitors each year since its dedication.

CHAPTER 005

INTO THE UNKNOWN

As they returned, night fell on the staging area in Angoville-Au-Plain. Word that the 2nd Battalion had secured Sainte-Marie-du-Mont spread like wildfire throughout the ranks. Elements of the 4th Division were beginning to move men and equipment inland from the beaches. Meanwhile, M4 Sherman tanks rolled through town, and men loaded up the five-ton trucks that had made it off Omaha's sandy grave.

Even though the majority of the 101st were still scattered all over Normandy, they were all ordered to pack their belongings. The members of Dog Company were preparing to move out again.

One of the privates walked the lines, asking the men if any of them had mail they wanted to send out before they got back into the fight. Several did and slipped the soldier letters, small packages, or even postcards made from pieces of cardboard — anything to get word home that they were still alive.

Donovan rolled Anness's blanket into a ball. He stuffed it and the rest of the sergeant's personal belongings into a cardboard box.

Peretti looked over at him. "Sarge's stuff?" he asked.

Donovan nodded. "Yeah," the private replied. "I thought his Jenny would want it."

"Thoughtful of you," said Peretti.

Donovan tied the package with a string. As he turned over his wrist to knot it, the young private caught a glimpse of the watch his father had given him.

"Crap!" he said as he eyed its face. The watch itself was still ticking, keeping perfect time, but the glass was cracked.

Removing it, he flipped it over and read the inscription again:

"Don't count every hour in the day; make every hour in the day count."

A slight grin curled his lips. Donovan finally understood its meaning as he placed the watch in a small box of his own and sealed it with a freshly written letter.

Confused, Peretti nodded at the package.

"What're you doing with your watch?" he said.

"In case I don't make it," Donovan replied. "I want Renee to have it."

"Why?" Peretti asked.

"I want her to remember me not as the man everyone thought me to be," said Donovan, "but the man I actually became."

Peretti smiled. "A little worse for wear, but still alive?"

"Something like that, yeah," said the private.

"All right, people, let's move out!" shouted Lieutenant Spears, jumping into the front seat of a Willy Jeep. "Coup de Ville isn't going to free itself!"

Scrambling, men began leaping into trucks as Donovan and Peretti piled into the back of a M3 Half-track. Looking out at the organized chaos, Donovan spotted the private gathering the mail and called him over. Handing him the packages, he thanked the young man. Then he settled back into his seat.

The young private looked up at him. "Where y'all off to now?" he asked.

Donovan looked up at the night's sky, flashes of fire illuminating the darkness.

"Listen." Donovan smiled and pointed toward the sound of cannon fire in the distance. "That-a-way," he said.

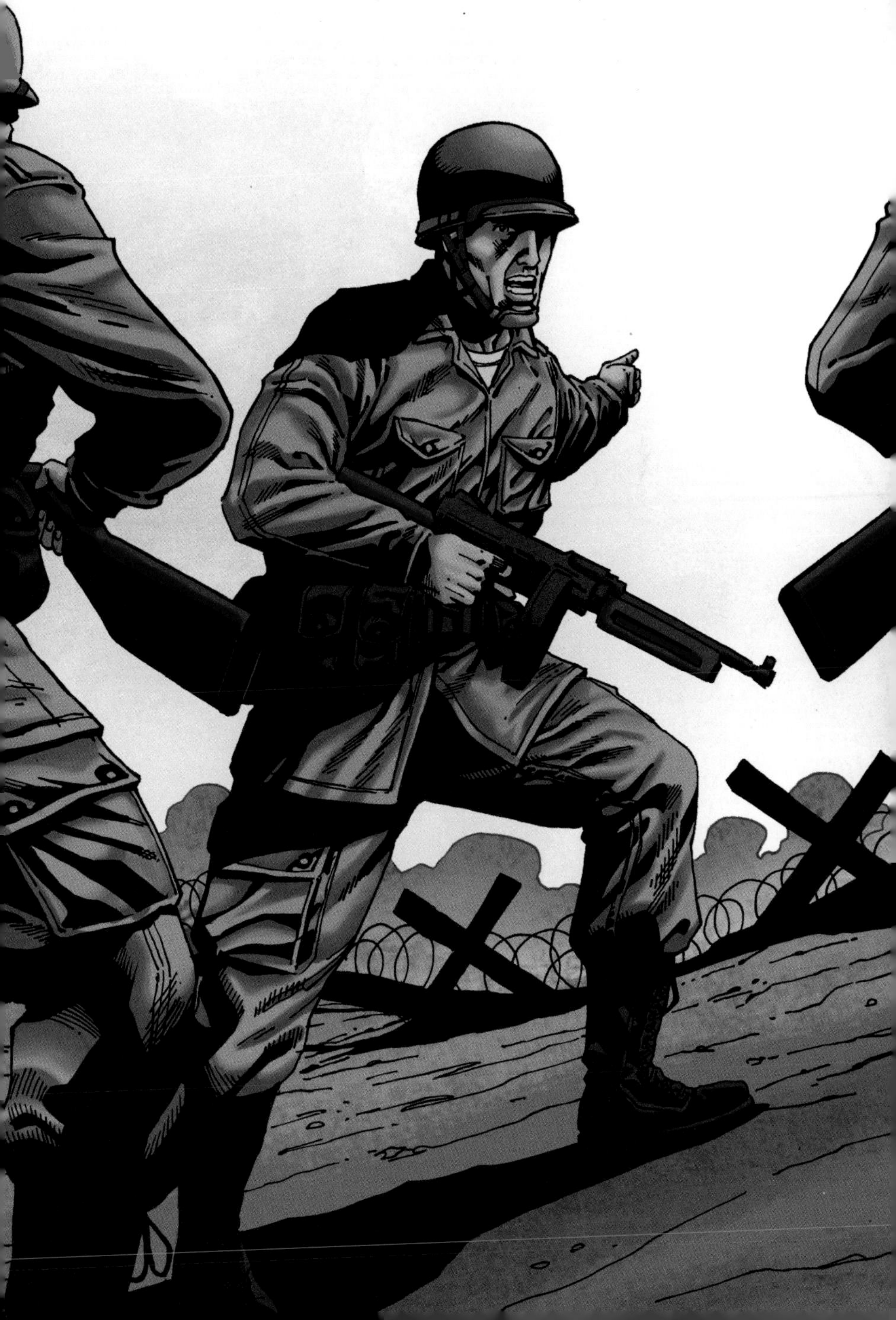

DEBRIEFING

M4 SHERMAN TANK

SPECIFICATIONS

SERVICE: 1942-1955
LENGTH: 19 feet 2 inches
WIDTH: 8 feet 7 inches
HEIGHT: 9 feet
WEIGHT: 66,800 lbs.
SPEED: 25-30 mph
RANGE: 120 miles
ACCOMMODATION: 5 crew
members (commander, gunner,
loader, driver, co-driver)

FACT

A device called a gyrostabilizer
allowed the M4's 75-mm gun to
fire accurately on the move.

HISTORY

The United States built nearly 50,000
M4, or Medium Tanks, during World
War II. The M4 Sherman, named
after Civil War Union General William
Tecumseh Sherman, quickly became
an effective weapon for the U.S.
and other Allied forces. The M4 was
reliable, easy to maintain, and fast. Its
main 75-mm gun could fire accurately
in any direction, even while moving.
Unfortunately, this weapon could not
penetrate the armor of heavier tanks,
such as the German Panther and
Tiger. Even so, the M4 remained an
important vehicle in the U.S. military
for years to come.

INVASION OF NORMANDY

HISTORY

On July 6, 1944, more than 160,000 U.S. troops and other Allied soldiers stormed the beaches of Normandy, France. They attempted to overtake German strongholds in the area. After many casualties, including nearly 2,500 U.S. soldiers, they succeeded. That date, now known as D-Day, became a turning point in the war. During the next year, Allied forces continued to regain territory and push the German army back within its borders. On April 30, 1945, realizing he had lost, Adolf Hitler killed himself. A week later, the war in Europe was officially over.

SURRENDER

Even as the war in Europe ended, battles continued to rage in the Pacific Ocean. Japan, who had attacked Pearl Harbor, Hawaii, in December 1941, refused to give up. Even after heavy losses, Japanese soldiers continued to fight. Then, in August 1945, the United States dropped atomic bombs on the Japanese cities of Hiroshima and Nagasaki. More than 100,000 people were killed. But Japan surrendered. On September 2, 1945, World War II was officially over.

EXTRAS

THE DONOVAN FAMILY

Like many real-life soldiers, the Donovan family has a history of military service. Trace their courage, tradition, and loyalty through the ages, and read other stories of these American heroes.

Renee Woodsworth
1925-1988

Michael Donovan
1926-1979

Military Rank: PFC
World War II
featured in *A Time for War*

Robert Donovan
1907-1956

Richard Lemke
1933-2001

Lillian Garvey
1905-1941

Mary Ann Donovan
1929-1988

Marcy Jacobson
1918-1941

Everett Donovan
1932-1951

Military Rank: CAPT
Korean War
featured in *Blood Brotherhood*

John Donovan
1946-2010

Terry Donovan
1971-present

Harriet Winslow
1949-present

Elizabeth Jackson
1973-present

Tamara Donovan
1948-1965

Robert Donovan
1976-present

Steven Donovan
1952-present

Katherine Donovan
1980-present

Michael Lemke
1954-present

Donald Lemke
1978-present

Jacqueline Kriesel
1954-present

Amy Jordan
1984-present

Verner Donovan
1951-present

Military Rank: LT
War in Vietnam
featured in *Fighting Phantoms*

Lester Donovan
1972-present

Military Rank: LCDR
War in Afghanistan
featured in *Control Under Fire*

Jenny Dahl
1953-2004

EXTRAS

ABOUT THE AUTHOR

M. ZACHARY SHERMAN is a veteran of the United States Marine Corps. He has written comics for Marvel, Radical, Image, and Dark Horse. His recent work includes *America's Army: The Graphic Novel, Earp: Saint for Sinners,* and the second book in the SOCOM: SEAL Team Seven trilogy.

AUTHOR Q&A

Q: Any relation to the Civil War Union General William Tecumseh Sherman?

A: Yes, indeed! I was one of the only members of my family lineage to not have some kind of active duty military participation — until I joined the U.S. Marines at age 28.

Q: Why did you decide to join the U.S. Marine Corps? How did the experience change you?

A: I had been working at the same job for a while when I thought I needed to start giving back. The biggest change for me was the ability to see something greater than myself; I got a real sense of the world going on outside of just my immediate, selfish surroundings. The Marines helped me to grow up a lot. They taught me the focus and discipline that helped get me where I am today.

Q: When did you decide to become a writer?

A: I've been writing all my life, but the first professional gig I ever had was a screenplay for Illya Salkind (*Superman* 1-3) back in 1995. But it was a secondary profession, with small assignments here and there, and it wasn't until around 2005 that I began to get serious.

Q: Has your military experience affected your writing?

A: Absolutely, especially the discipline I have obtained. Time management is key when working on projects, so you must be able to govern yourself. In regards to story, I've met and been with many different people, which enabled me to become a better storyteller through character.

Q: Describe your approach to the Bloodlines series. Did personal experiences in the military influence the stories?

A: Yes and no. I didn't have these types of experiences in the military, but the characters are based on real people I've encountered. And those scenarios are all real, just the characters we follow have been inserted into the time lines. I wanted the stories to fit into real history, real battles, but have characters we may not have heard of be the focus of those stories. I've tried to retell the truth of the battle with a small change in the players.

Q: Any future plans for the Bloodlines series?

A: There are so many battles through history that people don't know about. If they hadn't happened, the world would be a much different place! It's important to hear about these events. If we can learn from history, we can sidestep the mistakes we've made as we move forward.

ABOUT THE ILLUSTRATOR

FRITZ CASAS is a freelance illustrator for the internationally renowned creative studio Glass House Graphics, Inc. He lives in Manila, Philippines, where he enjoys watching movies, gaming, and playing his guitar.

A CALL TO ACTION

WORLD WAR II

BLOODLINES
A TIME FOR WAR

M. ZACHARY SHERMAN

On June 6, 1944, Private First Class Michael Donovan and 13,000 U.S. Paratroopers fly toward their Drop Zone in enemy-occupied France. Their mission: capture the town of Carentan from the Germans and secure an operations base for Allied forces. Suddenly, the sky explodes, and their C-47 Skytrain is hit with anti-aircraft fire! Within moments, the troops exit the plane and plummet toward a deadly destination. On the ground, Donovan finds himself alone in the lion's den without a weapon. In order to survive, the rookie soldier must rely on his instincts and locate his platoon before time runs out.

KOREAN WAR

BLOODLINES
BLOOD BROTHERHOOD

M. ZACHARY SHERMAN

On December 1, 1950, during the heart of the Korean War, Lieutenant Everett Donovan awakens in a morta crater behind enemy lines. During the Battle of Chosin Reservoir, a mine explosion has killed his entire platoon of U.S. Marines. Shaken and shivering from the subzero temps, the lieutenant struggles to his feet and stands among the bodies of his fellow Devil Dogs. Suddenly, a shot rings out! Donovan falls to his knees and when he looks up, he's face to face with his Korean counterpart. Both men know the standoff will end in brotherhood or blood – and neither choice will come easily.

VIETNAM WAR

BLOODLINES

FIGHTING PHANTOMS

M. ZACHARY SHERMAN

late 1970, Lieutenant Verner
Donovan sits aboard an aircraft
carrier, waiting to fly his F-4 Phantom
over Vietnam. He's the lead roll for
the next hop and eager to help the
U.S. troops on the ground. Suddenly,
the call comes in – a Marine
unit requires air support! Within
moments, Donovan and other pilots
are in their birds and into the skies.
Soon, however, a dogfight with MiG
fighter planes takes a turn for the
worse, and the lieutenant ejects over
enemy territory. His copilot is injured
in the fall, and Donovan must make a
difficult decision: to save his friend,
he must first leave him behind.

AFGHANISTAN

BLOODLINES

CONTROL UNDER FIRE

M. ZACHARY SHERMAN

Technology and air superiority
equals success in modern warfare.
But even during the War in
Afghanistan, satellite recon and
smart bombs cannot replace soldiers
on the ground. When a SEAL team
Seahawk helicopter goes down in
the icy mountains of Kandahar,
Lieutenant Commander Lester
Donovan must make a difficult
decision: follow orders or go "off
mission" and save his fellow soldiers.
With Taliban terrorists at every
turn, neither decision will be easy.
He'll need his instincts and some
high-tech weaponry to get off of the
hillside and back to base alive!

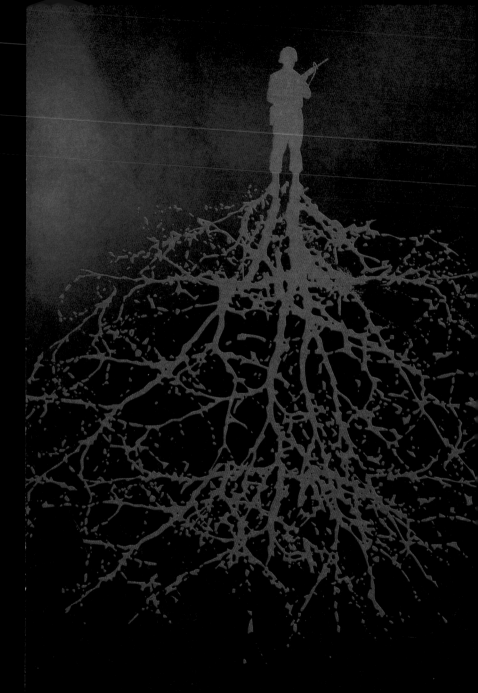

BLOODLINES

www.capstonepub.com